*Mentalist*

One who is believed to have the power to read other people's thoughts and place suggestions in their minds.

A performing artist who uses conjuring tricks to simulate supernatural mental powers.

D0528381

# 1.

In its heyday, punters might have filled the theatre and the air would have been hazy with tobacco smoke. But smoking and public access to the dress circle were both now banned, so the spotlight operator had the upper level to himself and his light left barely a trace in the air through which it passed.

Below him, he could make out the backs of the heads of the audience. Almost half the seats were occupied, which was a good turnout for this tour.

He looked along the spotlight beam to the man who stood centre stage. Harry Gysel, the show-man who was described variously as a psychic, a fraud, or a meddler in the occult — depending on who was speaking. He was thirty-eight years old, according to the biography on his website. The narrowness of his face was accentuated by close-cropped sideburns sculpted to follow the line of his jaw.

Tonight he wore a long, double-breasted jacket and dark trousers, conjuring an image that fitted the theatre's Victorian past.

He had already gone through the mind reading part of the show — telling people the jobs they did or wanted to do, telling them the makes and colours of their cars. He now had four volunteers on stage and was in the process of calling up a fifth to stand in line beside them. This one, a young woman, had eyes wide with expectation. The spot-light operator shifted the beam to include her. The other stage lights dimmed, leaving Harry Gysel and the volunteers surrounded by darkness.

'You've come here to find the truth.' Gysel said to the woman. His voice sounding intimate, yet clear even from the balcony.

'Yes,' she said.

He gripped her shoulders and turned her to face him, locking eye to eye. The spotlight operator narrowed the focus of the beam. Everything else in the room seemed to disappear. The psychic and his subject. One bubble of light in the darkness.

'You've been thinking of someone,' he said.

She nodded.

'A man,' he said.

'Yes.'

'Picture his name. See it in the air in front of you. Let his name sound inside your head. You're missing him, am I right?'

'Yes.'

'Remember the sound of his voice. Keep saying his name in your mind.'

She closed her eyes. Her shoulders sagged. 'He's gone from this world.'

'His name...' Gysel paused, as if waiting for the inspiration to come. 'His name is Peter.'

It was as if a jolt of electricity passed through Harry Gysel's hands into her shoulders. Her head snapped up. A breath of surprise rippled through the darkness around them.

'He's gone,' she said.

'He's not gone,' Gysel replied. 'He is here.'

'Here?'

'He passed over from this world. But you can still feel him.'

There was a pause. The spotlight operator tightened the focus even further. The bubble of light contained just their upper bodies now, which seemed to hang in the darkness as if they were projections from some ghostly afterlife. The silence lengthened, becoming first uncomfortable and then mesmerising.

'Do you feel him?' Gysel asked.

Her answering whisper breathed around the room. 'Yes.'

'Do you feel him?'

'Yes.' Stronger this time. 'Yes.'

'Peter is here. He wants to tell you that he misses you too.'

She had probably been crying for some time, but it was only now that her frame began to heave with the sobs. 'Peter. Oh Peter.'

The spotlight operator had seen this moment in the show many times, but this time was the best.

Gysel stepped back so suddenly that he dipped into blackness for a moment before the beam widened enough to take him in. 'There is another in the room,' he said. 'Another spirit. His name is… Michael.'

'Yes!' The voice came from one of the other volunteers on the stage. A young man. 'My father. Michael.'

'Not long gone.'

'Just two years,' said the man.

'He thought more of you than you imagine.'

'I didn't get to the hospital in time…'

'He wants to tell you how much he admired you. He missed that chance in life so he says it now.'

The man's face dropped to his hands. He too was weeping. And the hysteria was infectious.

'You have all lost someone,' Gysel said to them.

There were nods and murmured agreement. But Gysel had shifted his focus back to the first woman. 'There is another person in your mind.'

'Yes.'

Perhaps he could have said anything and she would have gone along with it at that moment. Or perhaps he really was reading her thoughts. Either way, Gysel was going with the moment, moving away from the usual format. People in the audience were standing.

'Picture the person. See him in front of you.' Gysel paused. The held breaths of the audience electrified the silence. 'Not a man,' he said at last.

'You are thinking of a woman. Picture her name. She's still in this world. But...' a longer silence this time. The spotlight closed in once more. 'But she is going to die?' It was a question, said almost in surprise.

'Yes,' said the woman.

'And her name is... her name is Debbie.'

'Yes,' the woman said again, her whispered voice, amplified and carried to every corner of the room. 'Yes. I'm Debbie. I'm going to die.'

* * *

The energy was draining from Harry Gysel even before the curtain had fully closed. He staggered into the wings and propped himself against a wall. One of the stagehands pushed past. 'Good one,' he said.

But the last bit of the show had gone very wrong.

There were moral questions about what Harry did. When asked, he would point out that the punters left happier than they came in. But with that last volunteer he'd made a mistake. He should have got her name at the start. Alarm bells should have rung when she said it was someone about to die. He could have backed away even then. Hell, the woman was so suggestible, he could have taken her off along another track altogether. She would have agreed to anything.

'Harry, sweetheart. That was the best.'

He opened his eyes to see Davina, his agent, approaching along the narrow corridor. She bent in to kiss the air on either side of him and he saw the makeup that hid the creases of her face. For that moment the illusion of youth vanished. Then she pulled away.

'What a show! You *must* do that again.'

'It was wrong,' he said.

'Did you hear the audience react?'

'It was unethical.'

'Has she got a disease or something? How did you know, sweetie?'

'I'm psychic,' he said. And then: 'Did we make much money tonight?'

She shook her head. 'The hall was half full. After paying the theatre and your overheads there's not much left. At least you broke even.'

Harry didn't ask what was covered in the overheads category. Mainly her fee, he suspected. 'I need some cash, Davina.'

'For something exciting?'

'I need to buy a mobile.'

'You've got one already.'

'It's for someone else.'

'Sounds interesting.'

She opened her red leather handbag and fished around inside it, the tip of her tongue running across her lips as she extracted a fifty-pound note. He reached out to take it.

She didn't let go. 'I've a friend who wants to meet you.'

'But I just need to sleep,' he pleaded.

Davina winked. 'She said the show was hot.'

For a moment he stood, dumbly, joined to his agent by the fifty-pound note. 'OK. I'll see her.'

Davina released her grip. 'Good boy. She's waiting in the lobby.'

'I'm just going to talk with her,' he said.

Davina closed her bag. 'Do you think that volunteer would do a press interview?'

'That volunteer — Debbie — you know she could sue us? For mental trauma or something.'

'Great publicity if she did.'

'I don't want that kind of publicity.'

'You want any kind.'

She didn't add that the alternative was kissing his career goodbye. She didn't need to.

'Is Debbie really going to die?' Davina asked.

He looked into his agent's eyes. 'Aren't we all?'

Harry woke with his face pressed against someone else's pillow. It was lilac, and carried a feminine scent. He tried to go back to sleep, but the light was on. Davina's friend was stepping around the bed, pulling a brush through her hair.

'What time is it?' he asked.

'My bus leaves in ten minutes,' she said.

'Any chance of a coffee?'

She scooped his clothes from the floor and dropped them next to his face. They were crumpled. She left the room. He heard the squeak of a tap and water splashing.

He was still buttoning his shirt as he stepped into the kitchen. He found her finishing a slice of toast.

She said, 'You'll have to find a café or something.'

He looked at her. She wasn't pretty, but there was something about her physique that carried a basic attraction.

'Last night…' he began.

For a moment she smiled. 'It was great.'

'Yes?'

'But, I can't leave you to lock up.'

'Of course. I'll get my shoes. Maybe tonight you could come round to my place. It's only a couple of miles.'

'I'm busy tonight.'

She was sweeping him towards the front door. Then they were outside in the chill October dawn. The road was still wet from last night's rain.

'That'll be my bus now,' she said, and ran.

Only after she'd gone did he realise that he couldn't remember her name.


There was a warm fug of vinegar and frying bacon in the café. The sun had risen above the slate roofs outside, turning the plate glass windows golden and lighting the steam that rose from Harry's mug. He often came here. The sound of the espresso machine and the chink of crockery were somehow comforting. He stretched, making his chair creak.

There was nothing wrong with café breakfasts. He'd got used to them since the divorce — even more so when he started touring.

The tours had been pub shows at first — a hundred and fifty quid in his pocket and no word to the social security. He could get by on that, more or less. Then Davina spotted him and he made the step up. This was the end of his second season with her, but so far no sign of the breakthrough. She wouldn't stick with him for a third.

'Egg beans and toast!' called a voice.

Harry put his hand up and a plate of food was placed on the table in front of him. He cut through the toast with his knife and pierced the runny yolk of the egg. He wasn't ready to give up the touring life just yet.

The café door opened and a man stepped inside, haloed by the low sunlight. There were people who believed in auras, to whom such a sight might have been a portent. Harry had believed in auras once. He'd believed in lots of things. He couldn't remember what that felt like any more.

The man stepped towards him. His hair was short cropped and greying. He wore an expensive suit and seemed out of place in the café. Harry raised a hand to shade his eyes.

'Mr Gysel?' the man asked.

Harry put down his fork and stood.

'Are you Harry Gysel?'

Only then Harry realised what the man was.

'You're a police officer?'

'Yes.' He flourished his ID. 'Chief Inspector Morgan. I need to ask you some questions.'

Harry felt off-balance. Chief Inspector sounded like a senior rank. 'I'm having breakfast,' Harry said.

'I'm sorry, sir. This is very serious.'

A picture came unbidden into Harry's mind — the face of the young woman whose eyes he'd stared into on stage the night before. 'Debbie?' he asked.

Morgan paused before answering. 'Yes sir,' he said. 'She's dead.'

Harry knew that the mind and personality were functions of the brain. The brain communicated with the body through nerves and through glands that sent out chemical messages, telling the heart to beat faster, the face to flush, pores to open. Each hard-wired response had its own name — guilt, shock, anger, love.

He was sweating. If he'd been connected to a lie detector, all the needles would have been jumping.

And his awareness of what was happening was injecting even more chemical messages into his bloodstream.

Other detectives had been waiting outside the café. They'd chauffeured Morgan and Harry to the theatre then backed off respectfully, leaving them alone on the stage.

There were casual-sounding questions about his show, about how he chose his volunteers. Harry found himself staring at Morgan's black shoes, which were dulled by smears of dried mud.

'Did you hear what I said?' Morgan asked.

Harry looked up. 'I'm sorry?'

'Do you have anything else to tell me?'

'It's a shock, that's all.'

'You said you didn't know her.'

'Only last night. In the show.'

There was a metallic sound from the dress circle. They both turned to look. The house lights were up, revealing the two levels of empty seating. The spotlight operator from last night was pulling a gel plate from the front of the lens. He waved, acknowledging them, then put the plate into a carrying case and walked to the exit. The door swung closed behind him.

'Do you get fan mail?' Morgan asked, jolting Harry back to the moment.

'Some.'

'Had she written to you?'

'No.'

'You don't need to check?'

'I don't get that much.' Harry ran a hand through his hair. 'I would have remembered — if I'd seen her before.'

'Did you find her attractive?'

'What's that got to do with it?'

'I'm trying to understand. I'd assumed you'd want to help. Puzzling, don't you think? You meet this woman, Debbie, for the first time last night. You tell her she's going to die. And within a few hours...'

'I do want to help,' Harry said. And then: 'How did she die?'

Morgan paused before answering. 'The circumstances are suspicious. Are you really a psychic?'

'That's my job. I do shows. I...'

'But is it real?'

Morgan had been shifting his weight slowly from one foot to the other throughout the interview, as if in some discomfort. But now he stopped.

Harry could see the man's locked-in tension. This wasn't the shallow questioning of a journalist.

A woman had died and Harry wanted to help. Really he did. But whatever information he gave would leak. The press loved psychic stories and they had their contacts among the police. Until that moment, Harry hadn't decided how much to reveal. Now he made his decision.

'I read minds,' he said.

'How?'

'I don't discuss my methods, but I could show you.'

\* \* \*

'How am I supposed to write that one up?' Morgan asked the empty theatre after Harry Gysel had gone. Even though he was a senior officer, he was still beholden to the computer, the Home Office Large and Major Crimes System. It had to be fed with reports. Every interview ended up as signals in its electronic brain.

It occurred to Morgan that there had been no one else present. If he were to skip the last bit, the psychic demonstration, no one would know. And yet it was the crux of the matter, the way to understand what had happened on stage the night before.

There were people who believed they were reading the minds of others but who were picking up on subtle hints of body language. There were also frauds and tricksters. All Morgan's training told him there was no such thing as a genuine psychic. He hated the fact that Gysel had put him in this position.

'What did I see?' he asked, speaking aloud again.

Morgan's mother had died two years before. Her obituary had appeared in the local paper. Gysel could have researched the matter if he'd known he was going to be questioned. But where did that logic lead? Gysel had been nervous. But when he started the demonstration, the man's demeanour changed. His face became calm.

'Is your mother still in this world?' he'd asked.

Morgan had shaken his head, resenting the question.

'Picture her in your mind.'

It'd felt strange staring into Gysel's face. The man's gaze didn't waver, though Morgan found himself blinking and shifting his focus from one of

Gysel's eyes to the other then back. Had he given it away? Had he accidentally mouthed it?

Gysel then reached into his jacket pocket and pulled out a blank index card and a pencil, which he held behind his back so Morgan couldn't see what he was writing. He then slid the pencil back into his pocket and held the card in front of him, face down.

'What was your mother's middle name?' he asked.

'Emily.'

'And you want to know if I'm really psychic?'

'Yes.'

'What if I was? How would it change things?'

It was a question Morgan hadn't anticipated. He looked down at his hands. Did he somehow want to believe Gysel was real? 'I just need to know,' he said

'Do you want to expose me as a fraud?'

'This is a murder investigation.'

'You said it was a suspicious death a few moments ago.'

Morgan reached out and gripped Gysel's wrist, turning it to reveal the under side of the card. And there, written in a shaky hand, was the name. 'Emily.'

*  *  *

Davina's name card gave the address of an office in Nottingham, but in the two years Harry had known her, he'd never seen it. She conducted most of her business in pubs and on station platforms. The tools of her trade were mobile phones and rolls of cash each of which she kept in that red handbag of hers. She always seemed to know what needed to happen next, though he'd never seen her write anything down.

Today their meeting place was a coffee shop on the corner near Leicester Market. He'd drunk most of his espresso by the time she arrived. She didn't order but came directly over and sidled into the seat next to his.

'I've sent out a press release,' she said.

'Is that a good idea?'

'Of course it is darling.'

It was an optical illusion — the afternoon sun catching her forehead in that way. But with the dark interior of the shop for a background, she looked as if she was glowing like a medieval icon.

'I've called someone who works for one of the tabloids — I can't say who or which, but he owes me a favour, so he returned my call. But he'll be owing me an even bigger favour after this. Because this story is going to run big. He'll call you. He needs to know the name of the detective who interviewed you. That's a whole extra slant to the story — psychic helps police murder hunt. My God it's going to be huge. You're going to be huge.'

'Davina…'

'I told you — you should have done something like this before.'

'A girl died.'

'And you predicted it.'

'She was murdered.'

'It's almost like you willed it to happen.'

Davina sat looking at him for a moment, smiling. She opened her mouth and closed it again. He'd never seen her speechless before. Then she leant in and kissed him on the cheek. Real contact this time. She hadn't done that since she signed him up two years ago.

'I've done something else, Harry. And this shows how much I believe in you. I've got a film-maker interested. Documentary. Fly-on-the-wall. You won't need to do anything different. Just be yourself. He'll follow you round. Cameras are so small these days.'

'I don't want…'

'Think David Blaine. Think Channel 4.'

'I'm not comfortable with that.'

'He wants to start tomorrow. Just give it a go. For me.'

She leaned in and kissed him on the cheek again. This time the corner of her mouth overlapped with his.

She winked. 'You didn't thank me for fixing you up the other night.'

'You want me to thank you?'

For a moment Davina frowned and the glow seemed to fade from her skin. 'Oh. *She* said it was good. And it's given you an alibi.'

Harry felt stung. Alibi was a word that belonged to criminals. But she was right. During the interview, Morgan had asked where he'd gone after the show. The question came out casually, as if he needed to ask it for the sake of completeness. As if it was a standard box in a standard form.

Harry had told him. He'd been with a girl, someone who'd come to see the show. No, he wouldn't have called her a groupie. He wasn't a rock star. Yes, it had happened before —

one-night stands with women who'd seen him on stage. Sometimes they did get a bit obsessed with him.

He gave Morgan the address. Harry could feel the man's distaste. Or was it jealousy?

'I wish *I* was psychic,' Davina said.

Her words jolted Harry back to the present. 'I'm sorry?'

'I'd read your mind.'

'I need her number,' he said. 'Your friend, I mean.'

'So it was good. I've got other friends you could meet. You'll be a popular boy now. Your star is rising.'

'I just need to warn her,' Harry said. 'In case the police call. And…'

'Yes?' Davina was enjoying herself.

'…and I need her name. I can't remember her name.'

'You bad boy.'

She took out a mobile, tapped a couple of keys then turned it to face him. The display showed the name *Chloe* and a number. He took out his own phone and keyed the details into the address book. When he'd finished she stood up and looked down at him, and for just a moment he thought he could see pride in her eyes.

After she'd gone, Harry sat staring out through the window at the people moving past. He still had choices. He didn't need to do everything just because Davina told him to. He dialled Chloe's number and put the phone to his ear. It rang three times before the pickup.

'Hi, this is Chloe. I'm not here now so speak after the beep.'

The tone sounded. 'Uhhh… Hi. It's me, Harry. Listen, I… uhhh… I need to see you. Have you seen the news today? The police talked to me. I guess they might want to talk to you as well.'

The phone clicked and she was there. 'Don't bring me into this.'

'Chloe… they need to know where I was.'

'You can't tell them you were with me.'

'Are you married or something?'

'Don't be stupid.'

'Then what?'

'Just don't give my name to the police. I'll say you weren't with me.'

There was a click and the connection was cut.

# 2.

**M**organ was standing half way up a hill-side, dressed in white scene of crime overalls, surrounded by rust-tinged bracken. Here and there, outcrops of grey rock poked through the thin soil. A hundred yards up-slope he could make out the stone folly known as Old John. A hundred yards the other way, and far below him, was a path along which a few visitors to the park wandered on this autumn morning, passing the police cars, vans and ambulance.

And at his feet, the body itself — a young woman, fully clothed, face down, one arm underneath, the other splayed to the side. Two wounds were visible. The first, on the left knee, had bled extensively before death stopped her heart. The second was on the back of the head, where angular fragments of bone protruded through a mess of caked blood and hair.

This was Morgan's second visit. The first had been at 07.30, an hour after the body had been discovered by an early morning walker. But since talking to Harry Gysel he'd felt the need to come back and see her one more time before she was removed to the morgue.

He reached down and touched the skin of her neck. There was no warmth left in her. He squeezed his fingers underneath her waist, checking again that the ground there was dry. He stood and stepped away, rubbing the small of his back to ease the joint pain.

Hearing a scuffling of loose stone, he turned to see a woman with coppery hair stepping over the cordon of incident tape that stretched between boulders and clumps of bracken, running in a wide circle around the body. She looked younger than him by a decade at least. In her mid-thirties, he thought.

'Good afternoon,' she said. 'Chief inspector Morgan?'

Morgan nodded and pointed to a box of white

plastic over-shoes. She stopped to slip a pair on then picked her way through the bracken to join him.

'Dr Fields,' she announced, offering her hand. And then, when he didn't take it: 'The forensic psychologist.'

'I've been touching the body,' he explained.

'Oh.'

'She was dead before 11.30 last night,' he said. 'That's when it started to rain.'

Dr Fields tilted her head to look at the victim. 'Too young to have her head staved in.'

'There's a better age?' Morgan asked.

Dr Fields' eyes flicked to him and back to the body.

Morgan pointed towards a marker some thirty metres down the slope. 'The attack started somewhere over there. We've found blood, presumably from the leg wound. It all ended with a frenzied attack here. At least two blows to the head.'

'Frenzied,' Dr Fields said, as if trying the word out for size. 'What about the murder weapon?'

'No sign yet. Probably a rock though.'

Dr Fields pursed her lips. 'And the body was left face down?'

'We've not moved it,' Morgan said. He watched her turn a slow circle, as if trying to divine something from the autumn hues of the bracken and the distant trees. He hadn't asked for a forensic psychologist to be sent.

He cleared his throat. 'This is a chaotic killer,' he said. 'The body left where it fell. An opportunist weapon. A disorganised crime scene.'

Dr Fields was facing him again. 'I'd say he's killed before.'

For a moment, Morgan considered denying it, just to see the confidence leave her face. 'A year ago,' he said, 'there was a body found in Swithland Woods. That's a couple of miles from here. A woman in her forties. Face up that time. This one is what — nineteen? And face down.' He pulled the latex gloves from his hands. 'A year before that there was a girl in Victoria Park. That one was twenty-two and left face up. In some ways they seem different, but they were all head injuries, and all in October.'

'That shows control,' Dr Fields said. 'A highly organised pattern. The killer waiting for an entire year before killing again.'

'But the crime scene is chaotic. It doesn't fit.

What made you think this wasn't his first killing?'

She started walking down the slope towards the marker. Morgan headed after her.

'You're thinking like the killer,' she said. 'Try thinking like the victim. She's slight. Vulnerable.'

They'd reached the marker now, a triangular plastic flag hanging limp from stiff wire. On the earth below it were the remains of a blood splash that must have dried before the rain started.

'Somewhere down there,' said Dr Fields, pointing, 'the killer did something to make the victim believe she was in danger. It was night. Think how scared she'd have been. Which way would she run?'

Morgan looked back up the slope towards the body. It was a steep climb. 'She'd run away from him.'

'A terrified victim tries to move as fast as possible — even when that isn't the logical thing to do. Animal panic. She'd naturally run parallel to the slope or down it. And escape lay back down there on the road where a motorist might have seen her. So you have to ask yourself what made this fragile little girl clamber up the slope, away from safety?'

Morgan watched Dr Fields, fascinated by the

woman's confidence in her own conclusions — reached after such a brief examination of the scene. 'I don't know,' he said.

'He was shepherding her,' she said. 'She must have been limping with that knee injury. He could have killed her right away. But he was enjoying it too much. Ever watched a cat playing with a mouse? He had to have confidence to take his time over it. That kind of confidence means he's done it before.'

Morgan wouldn't have admitted it to her face, but he could picture it all in his head, just as she described — the woman scrambling up the uneven slope, blood running down her leg, looking black in the near dark, the killer following with a rock in his hand, easily keeping pace. He could hear the panic in her breath. Driving her up the slope, prolonging the chase.

'Mornings like this, I hate my job,' Dr Fields said. 'Don't you?'

Morgan chose not to answer. 'I've got to go,' he said.

* * *

Harry woke from a sleep so dead that he had no

sense of time having passed since he lay down. He was still tired. Someone was hammering on the door of his bed-sit.

'Wait!' He slurred the word.

The hammering stopped. He pulled on yesterday's trousers and was buttoning a new white shirt as he stepped across the room.

'Who is it?'

The answering voice was a man's. It was too muffled to make out the words. He slid the bolt and opened up.

On the landing outside stood a middle-aged man wearing blue jeans, a black t-shirt and an army surplus coat. Two boxes with handles rested on the floor, one on each side of him. They were black and battered, with scratched steel reinforcing on the corners.

Harry rubbed away a grain from the corner of his eye. 'Uhhh… who?'

'Davina sent me.'

Harry looked at the boxes.

'My equipment,' said the man.

'Your name?'

The man started searching through his inside coat pockets. His hair was an inch too long to be tidy and was thinning from the crown of his head. He extracted a name card, slightly dog-eared, and handed it to Harry.

*Peter Pickman*
*Pickman Films*

In the corner of the card was a small picture of a movie camera. It was the sort of thing that could have been put together on one of those vending machines in stations and airports.

'The fly on the wall man?' Harry asked.

Peter Pickman seemed uncertain about agreeing to the title, but nodded anyway. He picked up his boxes by their handles and stepped inside.

'You won't notice I'm here,' Pickman said. 'Not after the first few days.'

'Days? How long is this going to take?'

'It's hard to say. Just ignore me.'

So Harry went to the kitchenette and spooned instant coffee granules into a mug. Behind him he could hear the snap of catches as the boxes opened. He forced his mind onto the purely sensory experience of pouring boiling water and inhaling the steam. It occurred to him that Pickman could be filming already. What, Harry wondered, did it say about him that he took two sugars in his drink?

When he turned around, the camera was on him. It was smaller than he'd expected. Most of the space inside the carrying boxes was taken up with padding, spare batteries, chargers and the like. Pickman was holding the camera at waist height, looking down towards the viewfinder. 'Just act naturally,' he said. 'What are we doing today?'

'We?'

'You won't notice me.'

'I'm not doing anything.'

'That's fine.'

'Can't you start tomorrow?'

'Your manager said...'

'She's my agent.'

'She said we'd start today. It'll be fine. Trust me.'

Harry didn't trust him. Neither did he like the thought of ringing Davina and complaining about her plan. So, when he set out for the supermarket at 10.00am, it was with Pickman following. He found himself taking a long time over each choice, aware of the camera just behind, aware of people turning to watch. At the end of the trip his shopping bags had none of the usual comfort food and ready meals for one, but were stuffed with raw vegetables that he had only the vaguest idea of how to prepare.

He loaded up the car and closed the boot. 'I've got some business now,' he said. The camera was aimed at his face so he stepped to the side. The camera followed. 'Turn that off please.'

Pickman complied, but he was frowning. 'Please don't talk to me. It doesn't work that way.'

'I need a break from it, that's all.'

'Where are you going?'

'It's personal.'

'I should be with you.'

'No.'

'Your agent said I'd have full access.'

'She was wrong.'

Pickman looked hurt. 'She said you'd say that.'

'Right.'

'And she told me to get you to call her when you did.'


The call did not go well. Harry complained that Pickman didn't seem professional enough, that the camera looked too small, that he needed privacy. The excuses seemed lame, even to him. Davina's reply was quiet. She sounded hurt. She didn't want to lose him as a client, she said. But if their working relationship broke down completely…

Half an hour later, Harry was driving towards his ex-wife's house with Pickman filming from the back seat. Or not filming. The camera made no sound and there were no lights to tell him when it was on.

'Can you point that thing somewhere else, please?'

'You'll not notice it soon,' Pickman said.

But the more Harry tried to not notice it, the more he felt the back of his head itching where the lens was aimed.

As he pulled up the car, the sun came out from behind a cloud. The sun always seemed to shine on his ex-wife's house. It had a U-shaped gravel drive and a semi-circle of lawn with a striped mowing pattern.

He rang the bell and waited. Then he rang it again. At last the door opened and he saw his ex-wife standing in the hall, blouse neatly pressed as always, a small silver cross at her neck.

'Hello Angela,' he said.

'You're early.' She was looking at Pickman as she spoke. He stood a few paces away, eyes fixed on the viewfinder.

'Twenty minutes,' Harry said. 'You're suggesting I wait in the car?'

'It's half an hour. Who's this?'

'This is... uh... Peter Pickman. He's...'

'Don't mention me, please,' said Pickman. 'It spoils the scene.'

'He's making a documentary.'

Angela's mouth made an 'O' shape. Somewhere behind her a girl's voice called out. 'Mum, where's my bag?'

Angela called back into the house. 'You stay there.' Then to Harry: 'This wasn't in the agreement.'

'Look,' Harry reasoned, 'it's my access time. I decide what we do. If I want to have a cameraman around, then...'

'No!' Angela was shouting.

'Send her out,' Harry said.

'Not with that thing on.'

'You want to take this back to court?' Harry was shouting too.

'We have an agreement. She's not to be involved with your… your work.'

'He's only a cameraman for Christ's sake!'

'And you're not to swear in front of her!'

'Send her out and I'll stop!'

For a moment there was silence, and then Peter lowered the camera. 'I'm not filming,' he said.

Angela wheeled and marched back into the house. A moment later a girl emerged, a day bag in one hand. Her dark hair was short and spectacularly messed.

'Hello Tia,' said Harry.

She glared at him. 'Nice one, dad.' Then climbed into the front passenger seat and slammed the door.

'Thanks for stopping,' Harry whispered.

'The tape was full,' said Pickman.

* * *

A murder investigation is a machine for generating paperwork. Detectives have suspicions, of course. And maybe they can use those suspicions. But if they catch their killer and make it all the way to trial and if the defence barrister can suggest to the jury that they followed a hunch somewhere along the line — that's when the trouble starts. What other leads were ignored? Why did the police decide to follow a prejudice instead of the evidence?

That is why paperwork is so important. It proves to the court that all avenues were followed and that no hunches were used. Even if they were.

As lead officer, Morgan was half-buried in paper. Two of his officers were collecting all available CCTV footage of the streets through which the victim might have walked. Two were following up people who had been at the performance, tracking them down through the credit cards they used to pay for their tickets. On top of that, the victim's mobile phone records were being gone through, her friends and housemates were being talked to, and half a dozen other lines of enquiry were proceeding at pace. In time the computer would swallow all the information. But only as fast as the data processing staff could feed it in.

Civil libertarians were always worried about the amount of information the state had at its disposal. Morgan believed that, given a deep enough pool of information, a state would drown itself.

He looked up from a pile of witness reports to

see one of his sergeants at the open door.

'You won't believe this,' the man said.

'What?'

'The victim — she was on file already. She gave a witness statement for the Swithland Woods case.'

'Why didn't we know before?'

The sergeant shrugged. 'Our victim and the Swithland woman went to the same church.'

Morgan's sciatic nerve was giving him trouble again. Little jabs of pain down his left leg. It always happened when he sat for a long time or when he got too tense. He stood up and put a hand on the small of his back. 'Find the church they went to,' he said. 'Get the membership records. Cross correlate.'

'Computer told us to do that already,' said the sergeant.

'And see if you can find any connections to Harry Gysel.'

'He's got an alibi.'

'Has it been checked?'

'I'll get on to it.'

'Yes,' said Morgan. 'Do that.'

* * *

Peter Pickman didn't seem to need to eat and he somehow managed to drink while filming, balancing the camera on his knees as he sipped. He didn't even relent when Harry took him to one side, angled the lens away with one hand and begged for a few minutes alone with his daughter.

The worst thing was Tia's mood. On their days together she was usually angry with him at first. The handovers seldom went well. She'd shout, then allow herself to be bribed, then melt, then he'd get a hug. And finally she'd start to fuss and mother him, making comments about the contents of his fridge, the number of empty beer cans in his recycling bin.

It was the hugs that kept him living.

But with a camera on, she was different. She stalked around the flat, not speaking. She opened the fridge, took in the raw fruit and vegetables, closed it again and moved on without a comment. Physically there wasn't much resemblance between them, but in character she was so like him — the way he used to be — it was terrifying.

It was in the upstairs seating area of McDonalds that Pickman showed his first sign of human weakness. The cups of tea Harry had been feeding to him all afternoon were at last having the desired effect.

'I need to... you know,' Pickman said. He put the camera down on the table. 'Don't spill anything on it.' Then he got up and headed for the toilets.

'Dad, get rid of him,' Tia hissed.

'It's difficult, love.'

'Do something!'

And then he had an idea.

Pickman didn't ask where they were going. Presumably that would have spoiled the documentary. He followed, still filming, as they left the golden arches behind and got into the car. He didn't comment when they parked at the cinema complex, nor when Harry bought three tickets for the latest Disney feature.

'Screen three,' the attendant said. And then, as they tried to walk past him, 'You can't take that in, sir.'

'I'm making a documentary,' Pickman said.

'No recording devices allowed.'

Harry raised his hands in a gesture that he hoped would seem believably apologetic. 'I guess we'll see you out here in a couple of hours.'


The cinema was dark and all but empty. A slide-show of local adverts was showing on the screen. Harry and Tia took seats at the back. He was waiting for the rage to burst, but instead she gripped his arm and rested her head against his shoulder.

'Why do you hate Mum?' she whispered.

'Did she say that? Did she say I hate her?'

'Don't you?'

'It's not that simple,' he said.

'That's what you and Mum always say when you're wrong.'

'When your mum left me…'

'She said you left her.'

He stared at a slide advertising screen advertising space. The world was going mad. Sometimes he could have wished it all to Hell. All but Tia.

'When it happened, it shook me up. I felt very low. I had to go to someone to help me feel better again.'

'A shrink?' Tia asked, a new note of interest in

her voice. 'Mum said you went loopy.'

'I was depressed. And it was a hypnotherapist. He helped me understand what was happening in my head. I don't hate her.'

'Do you love her then?'

'Love and hate are brain chemistry, Tia. Endorphins and Oxytocin. Understanding that helped me to be well again.' He felt her pulling away from him.

A couple with four children entered the theatre and took seats towards the front. The man and woman sat next to each other.

'If it hadn't been for my depression, I wouldn't have got interested in hypnosis. If that hadn't happened, I wouldn't be a performer now. Every cloud has a silver lining, you see.'

Tia turned in her seat and looked straight at him. 'Mum says I shouldn't listen when you talk about what you do. She says it's devil worship.'

'That sounds more like your mum's husband.'

'She said it too.'

There was a long pause before he could speak again. 'I've got something for you.' He pulled a mobile phone out of his pocket and placed it in her hand.

'Mum won't let me,' she said.

'It's so you can talk to me if you want. And she doesn't need to know.'

Tia's hand closed around the phone. 'If love is chemistry…?'

'That's what we are — machines to carry DNA. You're my daughter. I'm pre-programmed to love you.'

'But if it's *only* chemistry…'

'I'd die to protect you,' he said, hoping it was true.

Tia looked back to the screen. 'Don't do that Daddy.'

* * *

Ever since the phone call from Harry Gysel, Chloe had been on her guard, peering through the window before letting callers in. But this time she was late for work. The bell rang just as she was picking up her handbag, ready to run for the bus. She swung the door open without thinking, took in the two suited men, then tried to slam it closed in their faces. She would have managed but the one on the doorstep was quick enough to get his foot into the gap. His strength was more than a match for hers. He eased the door back open and waved his ID in her face. Not that she needed to see it. A policeman is a policeman.

'We're looking for Chloe,' he said.

'I don't have to talk to you.'

'Don't be like that. We just need to ask a couple of questions. Did you go and see Harry Gysel's show the other night?'

'Get out of my house.'

She finally let go of the door and they stepped properly inside, their broad shoulders filling the narrow hallway. She found herself craning her neck to look up at them.

'It's nothing to do with me.'

'But did you go?'

She dropped her eyes to the floor and their polished black shoes. 'No,' she said.

'He said he came back here afterwards.'

She shook her head. 'No.'

\* \* \*

The victim, Debbie, had lived in a shared house on Evington Road not far from Leicester University. She'd had three housemates, all young men. Two were science students — a bearded geologist and an acne-speckled chemist. The third wore his straw-coloured hair in a ponytail and announced that he played bass guitar in a band — which sounded to Morgan like another way of saying he was unemployed.

Morgan stepped inside Debbie's room, pushed the door to behind him, then stood still, eyes closed, and inhaled. Everyone has a scent. It comes from their clothes, of course, their food, their soap, their fabric conditioner and their perfume. It comes from all the things they fill their lives with.

He opened his eyes and looked. A poster of an angel suspended in the night sky above some trees. A mosaic of cards, photographs and newspaper cuttings around the edge of the dressing table mirror and on the wall behind it. Images of rock bands, crop circles, Celtic crosses and a picture of the Buddha.

He now knew that the 'church' the other two victims had attended was an informal gathering of spiritualists and faith healers. He wondered how those beliefs compared to the beliefs implied by the pictures on the wall.

There were a couple of gaps where photographs might once have been. He peered into the narrow gap behind the dressing table to see if any had fallen. Finding nothing, he lowered himself onto a plastic chair, keeping his spine upright and his shoulders back. Even so, he felt his leg twinge. A tired man stared back at him from the mirror.

He slid a drawer open and breathed her scent again, stronger this time. Socks, pants, tights — all stuffed and jumbled together. He closed the drawer and opened another. A brush still tangled with hair, a dryer and plastic clips, a packet of auburn dye.

He sat in silence for a moment, then turned to look at the door through which he'd entered. There was a gap at the bottom. He could see a thin strip of sunlight shining through from the hall. And a shadow. The shadow moved.

'Why don't you come in,' Morgan said, keeping his voice easy.

There was a pause before the shadow shifted again. A moment of decision, perhaps. Morgan watched as the door opened and one of Debbie's housemates stepped inside. It was the musician.

'What do they call you?' Morgan asked.

'Diablo,' he said. 'I'm David, see. Di. It's a kind of joke.'

Morgan gestured to the bed. 'Sit.'

'It doesn't seem right," Diablo said, but he sat anyway.

'Do you believe in all this — angels and stone circles?'

Diablo's eyes jumped to the poster. 'Not like Debbie. She was… she was really into it.'

'And you're not?'

'The band is. It's our image. We're the Witch Kings.'

Morgan felt as if he was expected to recognise the name. 'Do you have a record? An album, I mean.'

'We sell downloads.'

'You've heard of Harry Gysel?'

Diablo nodded.

'Do you think he's a genuine psychic?'

'Well he's got to be, right? After what he did.'

'I thought you didn't believe in that sort of thing.'

'Not all of it.'

'But…?'

'Harry Gysel — he's different.'

'You've seen him then?'

Diablo rubbed his forehead, as if trying to ease

a headache. Then Morgan's phone rang. He pulled it from his pocket, standing up as he put it to his ear.

'Sir, I checked Gysel's alibi.' It was one of the sergeants speaking. 'We went to see the woman he said he spent the night with.'

Morgan's eyes were fixed on Diablo. 'And?'

'She says she hasn't seen him.'

Sometimes you hope for a bit of news so much that when it comes, you can't trust that you've heard it right.

Morgan swallowed. 'Say again please.'

'She won't back up Gysel's story. But I think there's a reason, sir. She gave a false alibi for a boyfriend once before. She's got a conviction for perverting the course of justice. I think maybe she's scared.'

Diablo kept still. Could he hear the other side of the conversation? It didn't matter now. Morgan was sure he had his man.

'I'll be back at the station in 30 minutes,' he said. 'Have someone bring Gysel in for questioning.'

When Morgan arrived at the station he was handed another gift — news of two connections that had previously been missed in the mass of paperwork. They must have seemed irrelevant in the earlier murder investigations, but reading them now, Morgan felt the skin on the back of his neck tingle.

He was standing in the corridor outside the interview room, armed with two photographs. To make an arrest he needed 'reasonable suspicion' — something more than the growing list of circumstantial evidence connecting Gysel to the murder. A lie perhaps. Then he could sweat his suspect in a cell while they searched his flat and his car. They'd turn up something. He was sure of it.

He checked his watch. Gysel had been waiting for ten minutes. He snapped the door open, marched inside, took a seat opposite the suspect and placed the photos face down on the table.

Gysel leaned forward. 'Where's my daughter?'

'There's nowhere safer than a police station.'

'Where is she?'

'Sitting by the front desk.'

'I'd like her brought here.'

'This won't take long,' Morgan said. 'The desk sergeant will keep an eye on her. You know why you're here?'

'Should I?'

'You said you were psychic.'

'I said I read minds.'

'So you don't have supernatural powers?'

'I can leave, right, if I want to?'

'Well, let's get to the point, then. Where did you go on the night Debbie was killed?'

'I've told you already.'

'You told us you spent the night with...' he took a notebook out of his jacket pocket and leafed through the pages.

'Chloe,' Gysel said.

'*Chloe*. Thank you. How did you meet her?'

'Davina introduced us. They're friends.'

'Chloe says she doesn't know you.'

Gysel's mouth gaped. 'I was with her!'

Morgan turned the two photographs over. Each showed a face. 'Do you know either of these women?'

Gysel glanced down then shook his head. 'No.'

'Would you swear to that?'

He looked again, for longer this time, and Morgan wondered if lying was something that Gysel was good at from childhood, or if he had practiced in order to do the stage show convincingly.

'Well?'

'No. Never.'

'This one…' Morgan said, tapping the photo on his left, '…was a fan of yours. She went to three of your performances two years ago. Another of your groupies?'

'I… no… I can't remember every face from every audience.'

'And this one…' Mogan rotated the second photo for a moment so he could look at it the right way up, then twisted it back and pushed it forward till it was right in front of Gysel. 'We know she telephoned you.'

Gysel's face was screwed up with denial and apparent confusion. 'When?'

'This time last year.'

'I don't know her. A wrong number, maybe.'

'She phoned you four times on four consecutive evenings.'

'I get… sometimes I get crank calls.'

'Why didn't you report it?'

Gysel pushed the photograph back towards Morgan. 'I've never met her. Ask her yourself.'

'She's dead. They were both murdered.'

Harry's face went slack. He stood. 'I'm going. I need to see Tia.'

'No,' said Morgan. He didn't have enough but he couldn't let him go. 'Harry Gysel. I am arresting you on suspicion of murder...'

* * *

Twelve hours later, Harry had been bailed and released. Eight of those hours he'd spent looking at the wall of a cell. The other four he'd spent sitting next to a solicitor in the interview room, answering the questions of a series of detectives. The same questions each time. Where was he last October? Where was he the October before? He'd been performing in and around Leicester, he told them. No, he didn't need to check. He began and ended each year of touring here in his home city. Always in October. Yes, he did sometimes get obsessive fans. Yes, they were usually women.

When he finally emerged from the police station, Peter Pickman was waiting, camera at the ready. Strangely, Harry felt grateful.

'I need a shave,' he said.

'Was that really bad?' Pickman asked. It was the

first time Harry had heard him speak other than about the documentary.

'Really bad,' Harry said. 'Did you see who came to take Tia?'

'Your ex-wife. I'm sorry.'

Harry wanted to drive across town straight away, to get his daughter back. He still had another half day of access time. But Pickman suggested a detour. Home for a shave and a fresh shirt. Time for a cup of coffee on the way.

Perhaps it was the enormity of what was happening to him, or perhaps it was Pickman's ability to be there without drawing attention to himself, but Harry caught himself not minding the camera any more.

'How did Davina find you?' he asked.

'She didn't,' Pickman said, still looking through the viewfinder. 'I approached her.'

Harry nodded. It was no surprise that his agent had been economical with the truth.

By the time they crunched to a stop on Angela's gravel drive he hardly noticed. He advanced from the car towards the front door, leaving Pickman filming through the passenger side window.

She was there, glaring at him, before his finger reached the bell. 'You've got a nerve showing up here.'

'I've still got 8 hours,' he said.

'You left her sitting in a police station!'

'There's no safer place.'

'I know about your girlfriend,' Angela said. 'You think I'd let you take Tia home to a woman like that?'

'Chloe? She isn't my girlfriend.'

'I've had detectives here. Asking questions about you. They told me what you've been doing.'

Harry tried to step into the house but Angela spread her arms to block him. He shouted over her shoulder. 'Tia!'

'She doesn't belong with you.' Angela's voice was a hiss. ' I've been trying to tell you this for years.'

'Christ!' Harry shouted. 'You should listen to yourself!'

Angela flinched. He could see the hurt whenever he swore like that.

'You've never taken my hints,' she said. 'You don't want to face the truth.'

'What do you mean?'

'Tia isn't yours.'

He understood the words his ex-wife had just spoken, but together they didn't seem to make sense. He found himself blinking rapidly.

'We're going back to court,' Angela said

'We?'

She pulled in a deep breath. 'I didn't want it to be like this. But you're ruining Tia's life. She's not your daughter, Harry. We don't want you to see her again.'

\* \* \*

The thought of letting Dr Fields, the forensic psychologist, into his office was unsettling, so Morgan booked one of the larger interview rooms for the meeting. She was waiting for him when he opened the door.

'Good morning,' he offered his hand, which she took. Her grip was soft.

'You've had time to read my conclusions?' she asked.

'I have.'

They were sitting opposite each other. She had a copy of the report on the table in front of her. He placed his own copy to mirror hers. Her coppery hair seemed even brighter under the room's fluorescent lighting than it had on the hillside when they first met.

'I'm hoping you can clarify something,' he said. 'I'm familiar with the basic division between organised and disorganised crime scenes. When we spoke before, you told me we were looking for a killer in control of his actions.'

She folded her arms. 'The crime scene was organised.'

'Which means an intelligent, socially able killer. A sociopath rather than a psychopath. Someone with no moral inhibitions to killing. But in your report you changed your mind.'

'It's never that simple. And we didn't know then that all the victims were linked to Harry Gysel.'

'This is what I don't understand,' Morgan said. 'You haven't mentioned the possibility that Harry Gysel is the killer.'

'I do. If you read section three...' Dr Fields flicked through her copy of the report, then traced a finger down the margin of one page. 'Here we go... "Assuming Harry Gysel isn't himself guilty, I conclude that…"'

'Why assume?'

"'…I conclude that the killer is fixated on him. The killer may have specific delusional fantasies of a relationship with Mr Gysel and psychic phenomena.'"

She looked up from the page.

Morgan said: 'I thought delusional killers left disorganised crime scenes.'

'Not always. If Gysel was the murderer, he'd make sure the victims couldn't be connected to him. I think our killer wants Gysel to be involved — to know the deaths are related to him.'

'It could be greed,' Morgan said. 'The man is on the road to riches because of this.'

Dr Fields closed the report. 'Maybe you're right. It isn't an exact science. But I'd say you're looking for someone who came into contact with Gysel two years ago, possibly after a life-changing event of some kind.'

'Like what?'

'Accident, mental breakdown, loss of a loved one. Anything like that. When they kill again, the victim will be someone Harry Gysel knows.'

'Why not kill Gysel himself?'

'Killing Gysel would kill the fantasy. As long as the fantasy is alive, Gysel is safe.'

Morgan took a deep breath and let it out slowly. 'Is believing in psychic phenomena a mental illness?'

'Do you believe?' she asked.

'No.'

'Not in anything? Ghosts? Jesus? Love?'

'There is something I haven't mentioned,' Morgan said. 'Something Harry Gysel showed me when I interviewed him.' He began describing the way Harry Gysel had divined his mother's middle name. Dr Fields looked at him so intently that he found himself dropping his own gaze to his hands as he spoke. When he looked again, he was surprised to see her smiling. 'If he'd known I was going to interview him, he could have looked it up.'

'You must have mouthed the name,' she said.

Morgan thought back, trying to remember. 'Not the middle name.'

'Well, did you tell it to him before he showed you what was on the card?'

'Yes. But after he'd written it.'

'It's a Mentalist trick,' she said. 'Conjuring that looks like mind reading. It has to be. What you should be asking is why he thought Debbie was going to die.'

'He wouldn't tell me,' Morgan said. 'But I do have some news on that. We found out today, Debbie had liver cancer. She knew she was going to die.'

* * *

The Sorcerer's Apprentice, loud but tinny, chimed from Harry's mobile phone. He groped on the bed-side table, pressing buttons at random until it stopped, then fumbled it to his ear.

'Hello?'

'Dad?'

'Tia? What time is it?'

'You said… you said I could call any time.'

He was more asleep than awake but the half sob in his daughter's voice was like a slap to the face. He swung his legs out of bed and blinked, trying to focus on the glowing digits of the alarm clock. 'Are you OK?'

'You were on the news, Dad.'

'I know sweetheart. Where are you?'

'It doesn't matter where I am! They said… they said a girl was killed. Mum turned the TV off and sent me to my bedroom. They said…'

'Are you there now? God, Tia, it's three in the morning.'

'Stop fussing about me! They said you were arrested.'

'They just questioned me.'

'Did you… did you really know? They said you predicted it all.'

'I didn't know anything. The woman, Debbie, she thought she was going to die. That's all there is.'

'But you predicted it. You should have stopped it.'

'I couldn't.'

'Mum says I'm not to see you any more. She says you're no good. She says…'

'I will see you.'

'…she says it's your fault.'

'Then she overestimates me.'

'She says you call up devils.'

'There are no devils, Tia. At least, only human ones. And I'm nothing special. All I do is conjuring tricks. Please tell me where you are.'

'Stop treating me like a baby!'

'I'm asking because I love you.'

'You said love is just chemistry.'

'Tia, I'd do anything for you.'

'I don't believe it.'

'Tell me what you want. Anything.'

'I want you to be special.'

* * *

The press conference was Harry's idea. When he told Davina about it she surprised him with an embrace so tight that he could feel her heart beating. It was as if he'd agreed to convert to her religion.

'We could book that same hotel the police used for theirs,' she said.

Davina had an instinct for the mischievous that he almost admired. Holding it there would certainly goad Morgan and that was a satisfying thought. But Morgan wasn't his target.

'The acoustics were terrible,' he said. 'Anyway, I've got a better idea.'

And so it was arranged. Back to the theatre, the exact spot where he'd stumbled on Debbie's premonition of death.

News of a serial killer had attracted reporters up from London, including correspondents from the foreign press. Harry stood on the street opposite the theatre, his face concealed under the hood of an old anorak. He watched them arriving, jostling each other as they pressed through the doors. French and Italian accents mingled with the English. When he'd heard enough, he followed them in and made his way to the wings. There he took off his coat and waited.

Davina was standing centre stage behind a bank of microphones. He listened to her addressing the audience, priming them, telling them what to expect. She would have been a good stage hypnotist.

Then, at her command the lights dimmed.

'Good luck,' whispered Pickman just behind him. Harry stepped out from his hiding place. Camera flashes strobed him as he advanced towards the microphones. He peered into the audience. There were more people here than on his last performance. Then the stage lights came up full and he couldn't see them any more.

'Mr Gysel will take your questions now,' said Davina.

There must have been a radio microphone in the audience because the voice of the first questioner issued clear from the stage speakers. 'Harry. Are you using your powers to help the police or are you a suspect?'

This one they'd expected. 'Some people see beauty and mystery in the world,' he said. 'But it's hard for the police to admit there's more between heaven and earth than the ozone layer. I predicted Debbie's death. It's natural they needed to question me.'

Out there in the audience the microphone changed hands. A new voice spoke. 'Were you born with special powers or did you develop them?'

'We use only 10% of our brain capacity. We are all capable of amazing things.' It didn't matter that the statistic was made up. And it didn't matter that he hadn't answered the question. Play the mystic, Davina had said. The less you say the more they'll want.

'Mr Gysel, do you believe in God?'

'What I believe isn't the point. But there are powers in the universe that we don't understand.'

'Harry. What did you tell the police? Is the killer going to strike again?'

'All I told the police is confidential.'

'Give us a demonstration, Harry. Read my mind.'

Davina sidled between Harry and the microphones. 'Harry Gysel will be performing at venues around the country for the next month. A new tour list is on his website today. If you want demonstrations, that's your opportunity.'

Another voice from the floor. A shaky one this time, unlike the hard-bitten hacks. 'Do you... do you make things happen? Or is it... is it like everything's set?'

Harry peered into the spotlight beam but could make out no more than the silhouette of heads against the yellow haze. 'I don't understand the question.'

'Did you... I mean, did you make it happen? Did your powers kill Debbie?'

'What newspaper do you represent?' Davina asked.

'I'm just... I was Debbie's friend, that's all. She was my housemate.'

Harry could hear the movement of people out there in the audience. Camera flashes flickered, picking out a man with long hair, sitting half way back.

'What's your name?' one of the reporters shouted.

'They call me Diablo. I'm the bass player with the Witch Kings.'

If a girl hadn't died it would be almost funny — another wannabe celeb hijacking their opportunist publicity stunt. He could sense his agent stiffening as the cameramen on the front row turned to refocus on the musician.

He wondered who would watch all this tonight on the evening news? Chief Inspector Morgan, no doubt. If the man had disliked him before, he would hate him after this. Tia? Would Angela be in the room to click the TV remote?

Attention was still on the young musician, in spite of Davina's efforts.

'Diablo. What was she like as a housemate?'

'She was cool.'

'Did she believe in psychic forces?'

'She was like me and the band, we're all into it. We've got a new track out. That's about magic.'

Harry projected an image of Tia sitting in the audience in front of him. It was time.

'I can sense a presence,' he said, pitching his voice half a tone higher than before. There was a whisper of people shifting in their seats to face him again. He raised his eyes to the lights above the stage and spread his arms to stand cruciform. This was the image they'd put in the papers tomorrow. Angela would hate him for it.

* * *

Morgan had slipped into the theatre after everyone else was seated. He stood now by the wall on the left. He'd watched through the performance, taking in Gysel's agent, the hacks and then Harry Gysel himself.

As the questions came, he made himself watch the audience rather than the stage. Who were these people — all so eager to feed on stories of psychic phenomena? Then Diablo spoke drawing the camera lenses towards himself. Morgan hadn't noticed him before.

When Gysel spoke again there was something ethereal about his voice and Morgan found himself turning involuntarily.

'I can sense a presence.'

Harry Gysel, lit by the spotlight and surrounded by the blackness of the stage, had made himself into an image of the crucified Christ. As Morgan watched, the man's eyes rolled under his lids.

'I can sense… someone in this room… someone has travelled far to be here. I can hear a name… It begins with L. Lucy. Or Lucia.'

A blonde woman towards the front of the audience stood up. 'I'm Lucia.'

'A republican will reward you,' he said.

'Republican?'

Gysel rocked his head from side to side. 'I don't know. Republican. Republic.'

'*La Republica?*' she asked. 'I write for *La Republica* in Italy.'

'Do you have some old photographs in your house, jumbled in a box or an envelope?'

'Yes.'

'There's a picture of an old man. It is him, he's giving you this message.'

The woman was nodding. 'Grandpa?'

'He says you have been hurt in the past. He can feel your hurt, but you are healed now and it is time to move on.'

From where Morgan watched he could see the woman stagger back a step, then slowly sit.

Harry Gysel was swaying, as if about to fall. His agent stood open mouthed next to him.

'There are forces here in this room,' he cried. 'Powerful forces... I sense someone watching. A killer is watching. I'm looking into the killer's heart. There is emptiness inside. Emptiness and weakness and loneliness.'

Then Harry Gysel cried out as if in pain and threw back his head. His knees buckled and he fell to the floor. There was a moment of silence, then everyone was on their feet. The photographers were the first to clamber up on stage, then everyone was following. Everyone except the boy Diablo, who turned and walked out of the back of the theatre.

\* \* \*

Harry lay on the stage, eyes closed, listening to the uproar he'd created. He was aware of Davina's perfume. Her fingers were cool on his cheek. She fumbled his top button open.

Then other people were clambering onto the stage. The impact of their footfalls thundered into his skull through the boards. Their shadows were on him and the camera flashes were flickering. He covered his face with his hands and groaned.

'What happened?'

When he opened his eyes, they were crowding

in, trying to elbow each other out of the way.

'Harry. What did the killer look like?'

'Harry, smile.'

'Harry, is it a man or a woman?'

'Harry. Harry. Over here.'

'Will you go to the police?'

'Harry. Will he be coming for you?'

He let Davina help him into a sitting position. The crush of bodies pressed closer. Cameras held over heads pointed down at him from above. He stood. 'What happened?' he asked.

Davina took his arm as if to steady him. 'Mr Gysel needs air. Please back away.'

No one did. She started leading him towards the wings. The crowd was moving with them. Cameras were in front of his face. A long lens caught him on the side of the head.

Only when Davina closed the door of the dressing room were they alone. He dropped himself into the chair and looked up at her. There was a greyness in her face that he'd never seen before.

'What was that about?' she asked.

'They're reporters. That's what they do.'

'Don't be obtuse, Harry. What did you see?'

He stared at her, suddenly unsure. It hadn't occurred to him that his agent, one of the most materialistic people he knew, would be taken in by his act. 'I'm a fake, Davina.'

There was a look on her face that he couldn't decode. Was it fear? Sadness?

'Some of what you do is fake,' she said. 'I know that. But not all of it.'

He said, 'All of it.'

'Then how did you know the girl was going to die?'

'There are signs. If you think a word in your head, your face muscles shift. It's like you're saying it out loud. Some people can't help it. That girl — she believed she was going to die. All I did was lip read.'

He'd been planning on telling her the rest — that he was going to bring this killer, who was clearly fixated on him, out into the open to be caught. He'd been planning on telling her that the news story he was in the process of making would be so big that he'd finally be able to drop the pretence of psychic power and come clean and people would still flock to his shows. He wanted to tell her that she would be proud of him, that Tia would be proud of him.

But the admission he'd just made was already too much. He hadn't expected her to react in that way. Suddenly he felt too tired to move.

'I just need to sleep,' he said.

She opened her handbag, pulled out a creased tissue and dabbed it on the side of his head then showed it to him. It was stained with a drop of blood. She folded the tissue away. 'The reporters are out there,' she said. 'And they still want more.'

\* \* \*

It was six in the morning and raining hard when Morgan heard the news. By the time he reached Harry Gysel's place, four uniformed officers were waiting. He led them up the stairs, knocked once, shouted a warning and then let them break the door down. The place was empty. Leaving the men to search, he sped across the empty city towards the house of Gysel's one-night-stand, Chloe. But that was another blank. He drove off again, peering at the empty road through sweeps of the wiper blades, running red lights, heading for the only other place he knew of where Harry Gysel might hide.

It was almost half past seven by the time he finally crashed open the door to the theatre dressing room and found Gysel apparently sleeping in a chair, covered by his coat.

'What have you done with her?' Morgan demanded.

Gysel opened his eyes, seeming confused. 'What?'

'What have you done with Tia?'

# 3.

Time does strange things when you are in shock. Harry had felt it before — the day Angela, his first love, left him for the minister in their church. He remembered walking away from her in slow motion, turning back to see her in the doorway, baby Tia held on her hip. He remembered putting together the clues of her infidelity, thinking faster than he'd ever thought before.

Stumbling ahead of Morgan, the same lucidity came to him. Even before they'd reached the end of the corridor, he knew Tia's abduction to be the result of his idiotic bravado. He'd meant the killer to confront him. He'd meant to live or die as something more than a fake, to be a hero in his daughter's eyes.

He heard his own voice saying: 'Have you searched Angela's place?'

Morgan didn't break step. 'She's the one who told us you abducted the girl.'

'Tia is my daughter.'

'Save it for the station.'

Harry fumbled his phone from his pocket. 'Her mobile number... it's on here. You can track her.'

Morgan took it. For a moment he seemed uncertain, then he gave Harry a shove, propelling him towards the exit.

'Don't waste your time with me! It's the killer who's got her.'

'Is that another premonition?'

Harry wheeled on the detective. 'For god's sake! Help me!' He put his hands over his face. Time compressed even further. Thoughts poured through his head. Through his fingers he saw Morgan moving towards him, about to push him again. He lashed out with his arm. The detective was falling and Harry found himself running, crashing the fire doors, spilling into the lobby then out through the front entrance and into the rain.

How many seconds did he have before Morgan

raised the alarm? A car door opened on the other side of the road. His own car. Harry caught a glimpse of Pickman at the wheel and dived inside.

'Go!' he shouted.

Pickman was driving before the door was closed. The tyres screeched as they rounded the corner. Water was dripping from Harry's hair, running down his face. He looked out of the back window. No one was following.

'How did you know to be there?'

'I've been listening to the police radio,' Pickman said, steering the car into a narrow side-street.

Harry turned to look at him. 'Isn't that illegal?'

'Are you complaining?'

They parked outside a KFC, bought coffees and took them back to the car. The windows fogged as they drank.

'I've got to find Tia,' Harry said at last.

Pickman retrieved his camera from the back seat. It seemed as if he was going to continue with the documentary shoot, but this time he turned it so that the viewfinder rather than the lens was pointing towards Harry. 'You should see this,' he said. Then he pressed a button and the film started playing.

Harry saw the view from the wing of the theatre — Davina and himself standing on stage behind the bank of microphones. After a few seconds the scene cut to a view from the balcony. He saw himself taking questions. The camera swung left, picking out Morgan, who was standing next to the wall downstairs, then right again. It had that jerky, hand-held feel. Almost unusable, Harry would have thought, though that was the fashion these days. The view shifted to the spotlight operator on the balcony then down to the audience. The young man, Diablo, stood up and began speaking. Everyone turned to face him.

'What am I looking for?' Harry asked.

'Wait.'

He watched as the camera jagged back to where he stood on stage. He'd often practised in front of a mirror, but never seen himself like this. With the spotlight tight on him and his arms to either side, the illusion of being suspended in the air was compelling. He listened to his own words — his challenge to the killer. He saw himself collapse and the audience rush to surround him. The camera angle dropped. Diablo was standing in the midst of the empty seats. The boy put his hands to his fore-head and stood still for a moment. Then, as he turned to go, the camera caught his face. Pickman pressed a button and the image froze.

'See?'

Harry did see. The face was full of anger. 'I spoiled his moment,' he said, almost believing it.

'His band use an old farm to practise in,' said Pickman. 'It's out of the way. If he wanted to keep someone prisoner…'

'You call the police,' said Harry, 'I'll drive.'

Pickman directed Harry south out of the city. They were quickly off the main road, taking turn-ings on smaller and smaller tracks, until there was a ridge of grass down the centre and banks high on either side. Ahead, down a gentle slope, was a clus-ter of dilapidated agricultural buildings. A derelict farmhouse, concrete and corrugated iron animal sheds and a large brick building that could have been some kind of barn or machinery store.

'Cut the engine,' Pickman said.

Harry did as he was told, letting the car roll the last hundred yards. 'How did you find it?' he asked.

'After the press conference, I followed him here.' He pointed to the brick building. 'He went in there. Should we wait for the police?'

But Harry was getting out of the car already. He edged along the outer wall of the building with Pickman close behind. Here and there the mouldering brickwork had crusts of white crystals, as if chemicals had leached from the mortar. Overspill from a broken gutter was splattering onto the ground.

The entrance was a dark opening. He peered around the edge into a bare room with an oil-stained floor. Then he was inside, heading for the doorless entrance to what appeared to be an inner room, placing his feet, trying to make no sound.

He flattened himself against the wall. One step and he'd be able to see what was within. He made to move, but Pickman gripped his shoulder and pulled him back.

'Me first,' mouthed the cameraman.

Before Harry could think what was happening, Pickman had slipped past him and through the gap. Harry was already following when Tia screamed.

He rounded the corner and there she was,

standing on the far side of a bare concrete floor, face streaked with dust and tears, cuffed by one hand to a rusting horizontal pipe above her head. Diablo was nowhere, but still she screamed. Harry started stumbling forwards but Pickman had got to her. He turned and Harry saw two things in one moment — that the man's expression had transformed from apparent concern to angry contempt and that he held a Stanley knife in his hand, the triangular blade touching the skin of his daughter's throat.

\* \* \*

Morgan sat in the passenger seat of a patrol car, waiting. They were parked in a lay-by, listening to the stream of instructions coming through the radio. Harry Gysel's car had shown up on CCTV. They'd tracked him heading south out of the city. After that he must have turned off onto a minor road.

At first the radio messages had come fast, one after another. The trail was fresh. All available resources were being sent out to search. That had been an hour ago. Now the radio traffic was punctuated by long periods of silence.

They could have used Harry's mobile phone to track him, of course, but Morgan had it. And Tia's mobile wasn't connected to the network.

The car's side windows had misted, in spite of the air blasting from the vents. Morgan's driver turned the engine off.

'Keep it running,' Morgan said.

'What are we expecting?'

'I don't know.'

'Then what can we do?'

Morgan fixed his gaze on one raindrop from the many that were rolling down the outside of the glass. 'Do you believe in prayer?'

'I... I kind of do.' The man seemed uncomfortable with this admission, as if it might lose him respect. 'What about you, sir?'

Morgan thought for a long time and then shook his head.

'Do you not believe in anything?' asked the driver.

'I hope,' Morgan said. 'That's all I can do.'

\* \* \*

With a knife held to Tia's throat, Harry had had no choice but to follow Pickman's instructions, cuffing his own wrist to the rusting pipe above them and throwing the car keys on top of a small pile of Tia's things in the middle of the room. He then watched as their captor set up a tripod and a movie camera.

While Pickman was busy, Harry edged closer to his daughter, letting the loop of the handcuff scrape along the pipe until it ran up against a bracket. He was still five paces short but could move no further. Her outstretched hand was just beyond his reach.

Pickman turned the camera to face them. Then he stepped around it, closing the distance to Harry in three long strides.

'You're nothing!' he shouted.

Harry flinched, expecting a blow, which didn't come. Tia's mobile was on the floor. He thought back to Pickman's sham phone conversation in the car. He'd been a fool to believe the man had been speaking to the police.

Tia had stopped whimpering now. He could feel her eyes on him, as if she still believed he could perform a miracle and rescue them, as if his mental powers weren't fake. But fake was all he'd ever been — as a husband, as a father, always pretending to be what he was not, even to himself.

Pickman was turning the knife in his hand, completely focussed on it. He seemed to be gathering himself, as if preparing for his grand finale. Harry looked from the knife to the camera and then to Tia.

He tried to steady his breathing, as if this was just a stage show. 'Are you really a filmmaker?' he asked.

Pickman brought his face close. 'I can be anything. Don't you remember? You're the one who told me.'

Harry made a guess. 'You came to one of my shows.'

Pickman nodded. 'I thought you were psychic. You knew about my wife. But it's me who has the power. I didn't see it then. But I'm the one who was putting the thoughts into your head.'

Harry had done so many small gigs back then, they blurred into each other. But Pickman's words were chiming in his memory. A pub in Leicester. A man whose story had been a mirror of his own. Divorce followed by breakdown followed by what? Rebuilding? 'I said you had the power to take control of your life.'

'I make things happen,' said Pickman.

'What things?'

'I think it up here...' He tapped his finger against the side of his head. 'I think it up here and it happens. I thought it and those women died. I thought it into your head and you knew the same would happen to Debbie.' He held the knife blade in front of Harry's face. 'I thought you were like me. I wanted to show you. But now... now I know you're nothing.'

'Let her go and I'll show you something magical,' said Harry.

'You know she has to die. I'm the one with the power now.'

'I can... I can help you manifest your power.' As soon as Harry said the words, he knew he'd scored a hit. Pickman swallowed heavily.

'You could film it,' Harry said. Another hit. The man was nodding. 'You must have planned this all along.'

'Yes.'

'Undo my wrist and I'll show you.'

Pickman's slack face tightened and Harry knew he'd made a mistake. It was like seeing a curtain descending. Pickman turned and grabbed Tia's free arm. She started screaming. Then he dug the blade into her wrist and blood was trickling onto the floor.

Harry cried out.

'I'm doing you a favour,' Pickman said. 'She's not even yours.'

'Stop it!'

'Show me my power.'

Tia was pressing her wrist against her chest. The blood began to bloom into her clothes.

'Well?' Pickman said.

For a moment, Harry couldn't move. Then he put his free hand in his jacket pocket. When he pulled it out he was holding a blank index card and, stuck to his thumb, hidden from view, was a grain of pencil graphite.

He was sweating. He held the card up in front of Pickman's face, snatched a breath and said, 'You have power.'

Pickman stared at the blank card. 'What's that?'

'You have psychic power.'

Pickman screwed his eyes closed, as if trying to block out the confusion. 'She's still going to die.'

'There's a shape drawn on the other side of this

card,' Harry lied. 'Use your psychic powers. Read my mind. Tell me what it is.'

Pickman opened his eyes again. 'A… a triangle?'

Keeping the rest of his hand still, Harry started to move his thumb, dragging the grain of graphite slowly across the card, leaving a pencil line. If Pickman really looked, he might see the movement. 'Think,' Harry said. 'What would you do if you're right?'

'Dad,' Tia called. 'I'm feeling faint.'

Pickman whipped his head towards her. 'Shut up!'

Harry moved his thumb quickly, finishing off a triangle on the card.

Pickman was facing him again. He grabbed Harry's wrist and turned it. He stared at the shape. 'I did it,' he said.

Harry paused and then said, 'Maybe.'

'Maybe?'

'It could have been chance.'

'I can do it again!'

'You can try. I don't have more cards but I did send a text to Tia's phone last night. If you could read that message from my mind…'

'Do it,' Pickman said. 'Think it to me.'

Harry could feel his heart thumping high in his chest. Tia would play along if only she understood what he was doing.

'It's something to do with love,' Pickman said.

'Go on.'

'You said, "I love you".'

Harry pointed towards Tia's phone. 'Check for yourself.'

Pickman grabbed it from the floor, opened it and clicked it on. It chimed as it came on line. He scrolled through the menu. 'Nothing,' he said. 'No message.'

'I did send it,' Harry said.

'It would be here!' Pickman was next to him in one stride. He raised the phone and slammed it into Harry's face.

Tia shouted, 'No!'

Pickman rounded on her. 'Shut up! Shut up!'

'He did send it,' she said. 'He did! I deleted it.'

There was blood dripping from Harry's nose. He looked across the space that separated him from her. Maybe Angela was right. Maybe Tia wasn't his. That didn't matter any more. He knew he would give his life for hers.

Pickman was blinking as if trying to clear his head. 'What was the message?'

'He said he loved me.' Tia's face looked deathly white.

Harry's gaze jumped from her eyes to the knife and back. 'Why did you kill the first two women?'

Pickman took half a step towards him and stopped. He seemed stranded between his two captives. 'They were after you.'

'They were just confused.'

'They wanted your power.'

'Don't you know what it feels like to be confused?

'They... they were trying to use you.'

It was only then that Harry understood. 'You were saving me from being in love with another woman?'

'I thought you knew!' Pickman shouted. 'I thought you knew it was me. Until... until yesterday in the theatre. You said my heart was empty.'

\* \* \*

Morgan had been shifting in the passenger seat for the last five minutes, unable to relieve the sciatic pain jabbing down his left leg into his foot. He closed his eyes and tried to focus on the sound of the rain hitting the car.

Tension always did this to him — that and sitting for too long. But the pain served a purpose today. It stopped him from focussing on a doubt that he'd been incubating since the moment Harry Gysel had handed over his mobile that morning. Morgan had been so sure of his hunch. But what if he was wrong? What if his belief in Gysel's guilt was pulling police resources away from the real killer? What if the missing girl died?

He pushed the door open and stepped out onto the roadside verge, feeling his shoes sinking into the sodden earth. Straightening his back sent a needle of pain down his leg. He took a deep breath, turned his face towards the heavens and tried to immerse himself in the sensation of the rain spotting his skin.

Then the radio crackled with a new message. Tia's phone had registered on the network. They'd triangulated it to an abandoned farmhouse just two miles from his position.

He was in the car again, slamming the door as the driver floored the accelerator. One mile straight down the 'A' road, then off onto a road with no number. The car slid as they took the turn, wheels slipping on the wet surface. Morgan braced himself. Hedges whipped past, close on both sides. The speedometer needle was touching 60. They crested a ridge and saw farm buildings below them.

The driver didn't touch the brake until they were in the yard. They were sliding but the ABS kicked in and they juddered to a stop.

Morgan was out and running before the engine had died. Into the brick barn. Through another entrance. And there they were — Harry and the girl, chained to a pipe, her clothes soaked in blood. Pickman was standing in front of them, blinking as if dazed.

Harry was speaking — that calm, performance voice. 'We're connected. We always will be. A psychic thread runs between us. You can't cut it.'

Pickman raised his hand, first towards Harry and then towards the girl. That's when Morgan saw the knife. He made to leap forward, but Pickman's fingers were already opening. The knife dropped and clattered onto the concrete.

'Ambulance!' Harry shouted. 'Get an ambulance!'

# Epilogue

Tia and Harry were sitting on the theatre balcony, watching the seats fill up below.

'I want to know how you did it,' she said.

'What?'

'At the press conference you told that woman she had her grandfather's photo in a box. I saw it on TV.'

'I said a box or an envelope. Everyone has *some* unsorted photos stashed away. And I said an old man. She was the one who said it was her grandfather. That's what she wanted to believe.'

'But you knew things — her name, where she worked.'

'It'll spoil it if I tell you.'

'I'll keep it secret.'

Harry weighed the decision, then said, 'She was chatting to someone before the show. I just listened in.'

'But anyone could have done that!'

'Could have,' he said, and winked. 'What you should be asking is why Pickman didn't kill us.'

Tia's hand went to her wrist. It had been four weeks now and the stitches were out but he'd noticed how she still felt for them whenever she talked about her ordeal. A lot had happened in four weeks. Harry had become a celebrity. His new tour had sold out and Davina was walking on air. But most significantly, the publicity had scared off Angela and her husband from going back to court. Maybe Tia wasn't his biological daughter. The truth was, it didn't matter to him any more. It was enough that he loved her.

'OK. Why did he release us?' Tia asked.

'Because of what I told him.'

'He was loopy,' she said. 'You could have told him anything.'

'I could only tell him what he already believed. That's the only thing anyone really hears. His wife had left him. He'd had a breakdown, just like me.

For two years he'd filled his life with the fantasy that we had some kind of magical connection.'

'How did you know?'

'I guessed. And I told him what he wanted to be told.'

Tia leaned into him and placed her head on his chest. 'If people only hear what they already believe,' she whispered, 'how come they sometimes change?'

He let her rest there for a moment before lifting her off. 'I've got to go.' He kissed her on the forehead as he got up. Then he called across to the right. 'Keep half an eye on her, will you?'

'Sure thing,' said the spotlight operator. 'Break a leg.'


At last the house lights dropped. Harry Gysel strode onto the stage and waited for the applause and cheering to subside. 'Ladies and gentlemen,' he said. 'There is more between heaven and earth than we will ever guess. But what you see tonight will be illusion.'